EMERGENCY PILOT

EMERGENCY PILOT

AND OTHER ADVENTURE STORIES
Compiled by the Editors
of
Highlights for Children

Compilation copyright © 1995 by Highlights for Children, Inc.
Contents copyright by Highlights for Children, Inc.
Published by Highlights for Children, Inc.
P.O. Box 18201
Columbus, Ohio 43218-0201
Printed in the United States of America

ISBN 0-87534-657-X

CONTENTS

EMERGENCY PILOT

By Marianne Mitchell

Chris peered out the window of his dad's Cessna 172. Down below, the dry washes that cut across the Navajo reservation raced by under the wings. Here and there, a cluster of scrub pine broke the flat landscape.

Chris liked flying. He hoped someday he could take lessons. For now, he was happy being the navigator, checking their progress on an air chart. He had already located Humphries Peak on the map. Out the window the mountain loomed darkly against the setting sun.

"Glad you came along today," said his dad. "You can see how flying is the only way I get supplies to some of the ranchers out here." He added power and the small plane climbed some more.

Over the drone of the engine, Chris noticed another buzzing sound in the cabin. It zigzagged around them with annoying familiarity.

"We're not the only ones flying up here, Dad. We have a stowaway." He waved his chart at the insect and missed. A few seconds later, it buzzed by again.

"Ow!" Dad slapped his cheek hard. "Whatever it was, it just stung me."

Chris glanced down at his dad's lap.

"It was a bee," Chris said.

"Rats! Let's hope it doesn't bother me. Flagstaff Airport is about forty minutes away." He checked the instrument panel in front of him.

Chris did the same. A chill ran up his spine. He remembered that the last time his father was stung by a bee, his father's hand and wrist had become badly swollen. Chris wondered if the swelling would happen again. If it did, would he have to fly the plane? The only "flying" he'd done was on a computer, playing with the flight simulator.

They flew for a while in silence. Chris's mind filled with worry. The sunset on the horizon was fading fast. It would be dark when they reached the airport. He looked over at Dad's face. An angry red welt had formed just under his right eye. An allergic reaction was definitely beginning. Chris wished he could find some ice for his dad.

Dad winced with pain. The plane inched upward in the clear sky.

"What's the matter?" asked Chris.

"It's no good," he finally said. "I can barely see. I feel . . . woozy. We have no choice. You'll have to take over for me."

"But I can't fly a plane. Not for real!" Fear spread over Chris like an icy wave.

"I'll tell you what to do. You'll be my eyes and hands." Dad turned and gave him a pained smile. "I know you can do this."

Chris saw how swollen his dad's face was. He was about to get his first—and maybe his last— flying lesson.

"We're flying straight and level now," Dad said. "Our heading is good. Do everything smooth and easy. No jerky movements."

Chris took hold of the yoke on his own side. This acted as the steering wheel of the plane. He scanned the instrument panel. He was grateful it was the same setup as on his computer simulator. At least he knew what the dials meant.

He looked over at his dad. The swelling on his dad's face had spread, forcing his eyes shut.

"Keep the speed between seventy and ninety knots," Dad said wearily. "Can you see the city lights yet?"

"Yes," said Chris. Down below, the lights along Route 66 looked like a diamond necklace.

"Good," said Dad. "Find the university dome. It's a good landmark. Aim for that."

Chris's stomach churned. He had to fight back his fear. He had to concentrate on getting them down safely. His dad squirmed in his seat, trying to get comfortable. Chris checked the instruments again. Airspeed, eighty knots. Good. Altitude, ten thousand feet. Good.

Chris called the airport tower on the radio. No answer. He tried again—still nothing.

"The tower's closed," said Dad. His voice was getting weaker.

Chris let a nervous sob bubble out. "Stay cool, stay cool," he murmured to himself.

"When you see the dome, make a nice easy left turn. We want to come in on runway twenty-one. Don't worry about putting the wheels down. They're always down on this plane. Set the radio at 120.0. Maybe someone will hear you."

Chris turned the radio dial and tried again. "This

is Chris Michaels. I'm flying my dad's Cessna. He's very sick from a bee sting. I'm trying to land on runway twenty-one. Send an ambulance."

No response. The lights of the university dome came into view on the left. It looked like a giant ice-cream sundae with a red cherry on top. Chris started his slow turn and decreased power. The plane began losing altitude for the landing.

When he straightened out, all he could see ahead was darkness. "Where's the airport? Where are the lights?"

"Click your microphone button," said Dad.

He clicked three times. Like magic, the runway lights flashed on.

"Wow!" He checked his airspeed and decided to pull back on the yoke. Suddenly, the plane shook violently. An alarm blared at them.

Dad sat up. "It's a stall! Apply power, nose down, now!"

Chris's heart raced as he pushed the yoke forward. The alarm shut off. The vibrating stopped. He was in control again. The plane continued a normal descent. The altimeter clicked down by one hundred-foot intervals. The runway looked invitingly close. Pine trees swished by underneath.

"Bring the nose up a bit just before you land," said Dad.

They cleared the edge of the field. The wheels thunked the pavement as the plane bounced down hard and up again. It bounced one more time, then stayed down. Chris stepped on the foot pedals, braking steadily. Finally, they rolled to a stop. Ambulance lights flashed through the darkness. Someone had heard his call for help.

Chris slumped in his seat. "We made it!"

"Never a doubt," said Dad through a puffy grin.

BLACK ICE

By Crosby G. Holden

Amanda and Carol left the warmth of the skating shed and walked down the snow path to the river. Skaters in colorful costumes glided and swirled gracefully in wide circles. The ice was blue and thick here in a protected cove. Farther downriver, where the current ran swiftly, it never froze as solidly. It was called black ice.

"That looks like fun," Carol said wistfully, watching the skaters. "I wish I knew how."

"It's not hard," Amanda said. "I'll teach you."

Carol was Amanda's cousin from Florida. She was staying with Amanda's family while her mother was in the hospital. She had never seen ice or snow before, except on television.

Carol's mother had promised to buy her a pair of skates when she came home from the hospital.

"Do you think we could come down here every day?" Carol asked excitedly.

Amanda laughed and walked out on the ice. "Here's how you do it," she said. She moved her legs as if her boots were skates. "Come on, Carol. Try and get the feel of it."

Carol got behind Amanda and imitated her. "Hey!" she laughed. "Nothing to it."

"Wait until you put on a pair of skates and tell me that."

The two girls ran along the edge of the ice, seeing how far they could slide. Finally, Amanda glanced at her watch. They had come almost a quarter of a mile. "Lunchtime," she said, pushing up the bank through the snow. "Let's head for the bridge."

"Why go all the way around?" Carol asked walking across the river. She grinned happily. "We can cut across right here."

"No!" Amanda shouted. "Don't go out there. It's black ice. It'll crack under your feet."

"No, it won't." Carol stomped her foot. "See! It's solid as concrete."

"Come back here," Amanda yelled. "The river current undercuts the ice. It doesn't freeze that thick where you're standing."

Carol laughed and jumped up and down on the ice. "Come on, scaredy-cat. I dare you."

Suddenly, the ice cracked beneath her feet. It sounded like a rifle being fired. Amanda had only a glimpse of Carol's frightened face before she disappeared into the freezing river.

A terrible numbness froze Amanda's body. Her flesh prickled icily. Her heart slammed against her chest. Had the river sucked Carol under the ice? Amanda stared in horror at the rushing water.

Then Carol's red knitted hat appeared at the edge of the ice. Carol's face was white with fear. She tried desperately to lever herself out of the water with her elbows. No use. The fragile black ice continued to crack under her weight.

Amanda stood paralyzed with horror. She thought of running up to the main street for help. Then she realized that Carol would probably drown before she could get back. Even the skaters were too far away to hear if she hollered for help.

Amanda had to do something. She couldn't just stand there. She looked around vainly for a stick or a rope, anything long enough to push out to Carol. But, if there was anything, it was buried under the snow.

"Help me, Amanda! Please!" Carol cried as she desperately tried to hold onto the ice.

With a sick feeling churning inside her, Amanda realized if Carol were to be saved, it was up to her. Shedding her jacket, she slid down the snow-covered bank. She lay facedown on the ice and crawled toward Carol. She had read somewhere that was the safest way to distribute your weight on dangerous ice.

It seemed to take forever as she crawled toward Carol's frightened face. Carol clutched at the ice with her forearms. Another chunk broke off and drifted away behind her. Amanda crept forward another foot. The ice beneath her groaned dangerously. A cold sweat of fear bathed her body. She knew she couldn't go any farther safely.

Holding her jacket by the sleeve she tried to sling it out for Carol to grab. No use. It was about two feet too short. Amanda felt frozen in time, but she knew the clock was running out for Carol. She was as close to Carol as she could go. Her mind churned frantically.

"Amanda! Please hurry! I can't hold on very much longer."

Suddenly, Amanda had an idea. It had to work. It was the last chance they had. Cautiously, she raised her upper body off the ice and pulled off her sweatshirt. She quickly knotted the sleeves of her jacket and sweatshirt together.

Satisfied that the knot would hold, she whipped the jacket toward Carol. This time it was long enough. Carol grabbed the sleeve with both hands. Amanda tried to jerk her out of the water. The ice cracked under Amanda. Instead of Carol coming toward her, she was sliding toward Carol! There was no way she could anchor herself.

Some of the skaters had seen what had happened and were now on the bank behind Amanda. Amanda was afraid that one of them might try to come out on the ice as far as she was. Then, a pair of strong hands grabbed her ankles and someone said, "I've got my blades dug into the ice. Go ahead and pull."

Amanda pulled as hard as she could. For a moment, Carol didn't move. Amanda strained again with all the strength in her body. Slowly, Carol came out of the water and slid across the ice toward Amanda. Her face was still frozen with fear. Her teeth chattered.

Someone had called an ambulance and the paramedics wrapped Carol in a warm blanket.

"That was good thinking, kid," one paramedic said. "You saved her life."

Amanda looked around for the skater who had held her ankles, but he had disappeared in the crowd. "I didn't do it all alone," she said. "Someone helped me." She stared at the gaping hole in the ice and the swiftly moving black water. She knew she'd never forget that moment.

"Let's go," she said to Carol as the paramedics helped the girls into the ambulance.

Carol nodded and smiled faintly. "And from now on, I'll take the long way home."

The
Lifeline

By Eva K. Betz

Michael looked out the window at the snow piling up on the clothesline that ran from the kitchen door to the barn. As he watched, a sudden gust of wind came and cleared the snow off the line. It had been snowing heavily since early that morning when his parents had left for Providence. But the weather reports hadn't mentioned a blizzard, and it looked as if this was going to be one.

The telephone rang. "This is Dad, Michael. We found your uncle much better when we got to the hospital. Are you all right?"

"I'm fine and glad Uncle Lou is out of danger. It has been snowing ever since you left this morning."

"Yes, we heard, but the storm is supposed to stop by midafternoon. Of course, it may take us a little longer than usual to get home, but we're starting now and should be there before six. How are the lambs? Have you kept the heat on?"

"Oh, yes. They were nice and warm when I fed them at one o'clock."

"Fine. Mother and I will be along as soon as we can."

Michael thought his father had been about to say something more, but perhaps he had been cut off. He looked out and saw that the snow was heavier now. It was very dark for three in the afternoon. He tried to turn on the light, but all he got was the click of the switch. He tried another lamp, but no light.

Then he realized that the wires must be down. The storm had hit the valley first. Possibly the reason his father had been cut off was because the telephone lines were down, too. He picked up the receiver, but there was no dial tone.

If the electricity in the house was gone, it was gone in the barn, too. That meant the heaters that kept the motherless three-day-old lambs warm were no longer working!

Michael pulled on his hat, wool jacket, and boots and ran out the back door. Driving snow mixed with pelting sleet cut at his face and made breathing difficult. It was hard to see, and the barn looked very far off. A few steps from the door, Michael fell. The wind was strong, and the icy crust on the snow gave no footing. He got to his feet and reached for the clothesline to steady himself, but it was too high. He had to get the lambs to a warm place!

Michael staggered back to the house and ran to the front window to look for a passing car. Any neighbor would help in an emergency. But there were no headlights, and he realized it had been a long time since a car had passed. The storm was growing worse.

He ran to the closet to get his wool scarf to tie across his mouth and chin and knocked a wire coat hanger to the floor. As he picked it up, he saw the answer to his problem.

He bent the hook part into a very small loop. He shaped the part on which his coat usually hung into a long oval. Running to the back porch, he closed the hook over the clothesline. Getting a firm grip on the wire oval, he started for the barn. The ground was all humps and hollows. He clung to the hanger, and it helped him stay on his feet. It was hard going, but he made it.

The barn was dark, but Michael knew every doorway and corner like the back of his hand. He carefully made his way to the lamb pen and picked up one of the little animals. It lay quietly in his arms as he fought his way back to the house.

The second lamb didn't seem to like being carried. It wiggled its legs and struggled to escape from Michael's arms. But at last the lamb grew quiet, and Michael was able to carry it as he slipped and slid back to the house, hanging onto the wire hanger. The lambs finally settled down and drank their bottles of milk in a box behind the wood-burning stove.

Michael was exhausted, but he managed to get some oil lamps from the shelf where his mother kept them for emergencies. When he had them lit, he sat down to rest for a minute—and fell asleep.

At nine o'clock something woke him. The lambs were crying for more food. Sleepily, he warmed the formula, put nipples on the bottles, and sat on the floor to feed the babies.

Then he heard voices and the roar of a motor, which told him that the county snowplow and sander were going through. Soon the door burst open, and his parents entered.

"We followed the plow," his father said. "But even so, it was tough going."

"How did you manage? I was worried," his mother added.

"Oh, we got along fine," said Michael. "I got the lambs in with a lifeline."

"Well, you certainly have proved to be their lifeline, Michael," his father added. "You did some quick thinking, and I'm proud of you."

Michael smiled wearily, but he felt a new sense of warmth as he looked at the tiny lambs he had helped to survive the storm.

Out
of the
Storm

By David Lubar

It was supposed to be fun. It started out that way. Jim had risen before the sun. He enjoyed getting up when the world was still covered with a blanket of darkness and silence. He and his dad ate a quick breakfast. Dad talked about the hike, telling Jim what a magical place Teleman's Peak was.

"It will only take a couple of hours to get to the top. But wait until you see the view. The whole valley opens up in front of you. The view will take your breath away."

"Sounds great, Dad." Jim was looking forward to spending the day with his father. There weren't too many chances right now. Dad was working seven days most weeks, trying to get a project finished for the small company he had started last year. Jim knew his dad had worked extra hard to free up this one day. If it weren't for the thunder clouds, everything would be perfect.

"Do you think it'll rain?" Jim asked as they stepped into the damp chill of the morning air.

His dad looked up at the clouds. "I hope not. But if it does we'll just wear our ponchos." He pointed to the plastic raincoats neatly folded into packets on the backseat of the car.

As they drove to the state park, Jim began to see small drops splatter against the windshield. His dad flicked the wipers on and off every few minutes. *Please don't rain*, Jim thought. He held the thought real hard, trying to wish the rain away. But by the time they parked at the base of the peak, there was a light drizzle falling.

"Better put this on," his dad said, handing him one of the ponchos.

"Thanks."

They took their small packs and headed up the path. It was pretty in the woods. Tall hemlock trees and large spruce surrounded the trail. Leaves crunched beneath Jim's feet. The sun had risen, but there wasn't much light coming through the clouds.

"It's too early in the season for a thunderstorm," his dad said. "At least we won't have to worry about lightning."

"That's good," Jim replied. The rain was getting harder. The leaves became soggy and stuck to his boots. The temperature dropped and the wind picked up force, blowing the rain right into his face. He wasn't enjoying this. But his dad had been looking forward to the hike for weeks. He was working so hard that he was always tired and sometimes cranky. The hike had to be good. It just had to.

But the rain got harder. The wind got stronger. Jim grew more miserable with each step. Despite the poncho, he was getting soaked. "Dad . . . ," he began, not wanting to say it, not wanting to be the one to spoil the trip.

"Do you want to turn back?" his father asked after a moment of silence. He didn't sound happy.

"I'm wet. I'm cold. Could we . . . " He just couldn't say the words.

"You want to turn back, don't you?"

Jim nodded. Without saying a word, his father turned and headed down the trail. Jim followed. They didn't speak. Jim knew that his father was disappointed. They reached the car, still silent. They drove for a while without talking. The rain was coming even harder now. The wind whistled across the car.

"I just wanted you to enjoy this," his father said. His voice was flat. He spoke without emotion. "I wanted to share something special with you."

Jim was about to speak when the whole car rocked as though it had been slapped by a giant. It rocked again. For a moment, he had no idea what had happened. Then he realized that the force he felt was the wind. Suddenly, the whole world was nothing but wind and water. The rain came so heavily that the wipers made no difference. His dad pulled the car to the side of the road.

"Is this a cyclone?" Jim asked, beginning to feel nervous.

"If not, it's pretty close to one." His dad looked back in the direction of Teleman's Peak. "Don't worry; we're safe in the car."

Jim looked, too. It wasn't possible to see anything but flying branches. Jim heard a snap as a small tree cracked under the force of the wind. He was very glad to be in the shelter of the car.

"Jim," his father said. His voice was softer. He sounded more like Dad again.

"What?"

"You're a pretty smart kid. You showed more sense than I did on the trail. We could have been out in this storm. It could have gotten very bad. I'll be honest with you, I wasn't happy that you wanted to turn back. I'd really been looking forward to this. More than anything else, I had wanted you to enjoy the hike. I guess I had wanted it a bit too much."

"That's OK." Jim understood. "We'll get up there. And you've still got the day off. We can do something together."

"How about a hot lunch for starters?" his father asked.

"That sounds just about perfect." Jim settled back in his seat, happy just to be sharing time with his dad.

Alone * Under the Stars

By Marianne Mitchell

Patty gave her dog, Boomer, a pat as the camper bounced along the dirt road. This was their first camping trip in Arizona. She was glad her cousin John and her Uncle Martin had asked them to go along.

"Are we almost there, Dad?" asked John.

"Almost," said Uncle Martin. He put his hand up to shade his eyes. The late afternoon sun was right in his face. "We'll be settled before night sets in," he said.

"Boomer's going to love the desert," said Patty. The big German shepherd wagged his tail and sniffed the dusty air.

Uncle Martin turned off the road and parked the pickup near a sandy wash. They popped out the tent and set up camp. While they worked, Boomer ran all over, sniffing and pawing at everything.

"Keep an eye on your dog, Patty," said Uncle Martin. "If he takes off after a rabbit, he could get lost."

No sooner had he said those words than Boomer spotted a roadrunner and raced after it. Patty and John ran after Boomer, scrambling over rocks as they went.

"Ow!" cried John. He sat down hard, clutching his ankle.

"Are you hurt?" asked Patty.

"It's just a sprain. I'll be OK. You get Boomer. I'll go back to the camper."

Patty could hear barking up ahead. But the dog was moving too fast. "Boomer! Come back!" she yelled. But Boomer kept on running.

There wasn't any trail, so Patty headed toward the barking. Twice she spotted the dog. Boomer just looked back at her, woofed, and took off again. *A lot of good all those obedience classes were,* Patty thought.

Patty followed the sandy wash for a while, calling for Boomer every few minutes. Soon she realized she was in a canyon. Red stone walls loomed over her. It was very quiet there. Too quiet. She heard no barking. Nothing moved. The light was fading fast.

She climbed up on a small ledge and yelled again. "BOOMER!" This time she did hear something—an echo. Her own words came bouncing back to her. She tried not to let the panic bubbling up inside take over. *Stay calm*, she thought. *Head back to camp. Maybe Boomer will come back on his own.*

Then she gulped. Head back? Sure. But which way? Patty looked around for something familiar. All she saw were canyon walls. Several washes came together in the canyon. Which one had led her here? The sun had set and it was getting darker by the second. If she tried to find her way out now, she might get even further away from camp. She'd better stay put and figure something out.

Patty hunkered down beside a huge boulder. It would protect her a little from the cold night air. She tried not to think about staying out here all alone. She longed for her warm bedroll back at the camper. Her stomach growled. In her jacket she found two candy bars and a package of beef jerky. Some dinner!

Suddenly, she heard a rustle in the rocks nearby. A cold chill ran down her spine. Coyotes and mountain lions live out here, she remembered. They like to hunt at night, too. She grabbed a rock, ready to throw it at whatever was coming toward her. The shape moved closer. It looked like a wolf.

"Go away!" cried Patty, throwing the rock.

"*Woof!*" came the answer.

"Boomer! You scared me!" She threw her arms around her friend and was soon covered with wet kisses. "Boy, am I glad to see you!"

Patty nibbled on her candy and gave Boomer the beef jerky. "At least we can keep each other warm tonight," she said. She looked up at the night sky filled with stars. They seemed so much brighter and closer here in the desert. She picked out her favorite constellation, Orion. With its three stars for a belt and four stars marking the arms and legs of the "Hunter," Orion was easy to spot.

"Well, there's at least one familiar sight out here, Boomer. Remember how we would stand in our driveway at home and see Orion? Makes me feel like I'm back there." Patty lay back, closed her eyes and thought about her house. At home she looked south to find Orion. Orion, which always moved across the sky from east to west . . .

"Of course!" said Patty. "I know how we can find our way back. We were heading west, into the sun when we stopped. You ran off to the north, Boomer. That means we have to head east and south to find the camper."

Patty spent the next hour watching Orion climb across the sky. Now she knew which way led out of the canyon.

"Come on, Boomer. Let's get out of here." They followed the wash that led southeast. Soon they were out in the open again. A full moon bathed the desert with its cool light.

Patty checked the stars again. Orion to the south. Big Dipper to the north. She continued southeast, Boomer at her side. Soon she heard voices shouting her name. Flashlights bobbed toward her.

"Uncle Martin! Here we are!" shouted Patty. Boomer barked and ran toward the lights.

"You gave us quite a scare," said Uncle Martin when he caught up with Patty. "We didn't know which canyon you'd wandered into."

"Weren't you scared out there all alone?" asked John.

"We weren't completely alone," said Patty. "Our friend, Orion, was with us."

Ordeal
on the
Mountain

By Judy Cox

Snow. Everywhere. A blurring, blinding fury of white. I peered into the storm, trying to see the trail. Any misstep might mean a sudden plunge over the edge of a crevasse.

I thought back to early morning, when Dad had told me I'd have to go for help.

It was still dark when I stuck my head out of the snow cave Dad and I had built the day before—when we realized we'd have to spend the night on the mountain. Stars burned in the black sky. "It's clear," I told Dad, pulling my head back in.

Dad grunted as he tried to haul himself upright. "Lie down," I told him. "Keep that leg still." Yesterday, as we made our descent, Dad had lost his footing on the ice. I heard the sickening snap of bone when he fell. We bound his legs together, the way I had learned in my first aid course. We used the straps of our backpacks because we didn't have a splint.

It had been late in the afternoon and growing dark when it happened. There was no time for me to make it down to the ski lodge before night fell. Following Dad's directions, I scooped a simple cave in the snow. All night we huddled together for warmth, wrapped in our space blanket, snacking on freeze-dried food and melted snow. We waited for morning, when I could hike down to the lodge for help.

In the morning, Dad had looked at me and sighed. "I wish you didn't have to go alone, Margaret," he said. His face was white and drawn.

"I'll be fine, Dad," I told him, trying to sound cheerful. But my heart thumped painfully under my jacket, and my mouth was dry.

Now, here I was, lost in a blizzard that dropped from the sky with silent speed. One minute I was making good time, nearly sliding down the trail toward safety, the next I was wrapped in a swirling world of white.

Before I left, I had tied my red wool scarf to Dad's walking stick and jammed it on top of our snow cave. I hoped it would guide us back to him when I brought help. Now the snow fell fast and thick. Would the stick be buried? I hoped Dad would be warm enough—he had the blanket and we both wore layers of clothes, from thermal underwear to waterproof outerwear.

We had planned the trip together carefully last winter. "We'll go in the spring," Dad told me. "The best time is just after the winter storms have ended and before the spring thaws make the trail too slick."

The night before our climb, we had stayed in the ski lodge. Dad set the alarm for 3:00 A.M. We wanted to make our ascent while the snow was firm enough for good traction. The climb went smoothly. The day was partly clear and the views were terrific.

At the summit, we shared a snack of freeze-dried fruit. We started down in the afternoon, intending to reach the lodge before dark. Dad had climbed the mountain dozens of times. This was the first time I was old enough to join him.

We had prepared for cold. But we had not anticipated his accident.

Now I concentrated on keeping my footing, and I peered into the whiteout. Which direction was the lodge? The trail was completely covered—all of the landmarks buried in fresh snow. The wind seemed to blow first from one direction and then from another. I hesitated. Should I build another shelter and wait it out? Spring storms can last for days! To delay might mean Dad's death from exposure—or mine. I swallowed hard, turned my back to the wind, and inched forward.

Suddenly, the wind dropped. Ahead of me, the fog lifted and I saw a dark shape in the dim whiteness. Too straight and tall for a tree. The ski lift! I could have kissed it. Gratefully, I headed that way. I could follow the lift back down to the lodge for help.

Several hours later, I rode back up the mountain on an orange snow-cat. I directed Jeff, the driver, up the trail, and there was my red scarf, poking out of a snow-covered bump. "It was good thinking to mark the cave like that," Jeff told me.

"Dad!" I yelled, jumping off the cat. I dug at the loose snow with my hands until I broke through the crust of snow to the cave's entrance.

"Margaret!" Dad cried. I breathed a sigh of relief. He was still alive, but worn out with worry and pain. The rescue team checked his vital signs and slid him onto a stretcher. Then they hoisted the stretcher onto the snow-cat to bring him back down to the lodge.

"He'll be OK once we get him to the hospital," Jeff said. "No sign of frostbite." He turned to Dad. "You've got a brave girl here," said Jeff. "She's a real hero."

"I know," said Dad, squeezing my hand. Together, we rode the snow-cat back down the mountain to safety.

Last Chance
at
Lookout Point

By Frances Kane

The outboard motor coughed again. Bob adjusted the gas feed, and the bow of his twelve-foot skiff lowered an inch or two into the water. Bob spoke to his motor as though it were his friend.

"Skeeter," he pleaded, "be good to me. You know Jay and Sally said this morning on the phone that they would be ready and waiting on Lookout Point at ten o'clock sharp. They'll have the rope ladder already hanging over the cliff for me. And you know how they always complain if I'm late."

Almost as an answer, Skeeter coughed again, spluttered, and then stopped.

Bob grabbed his tool kit and made a quick survey of the trouble.

"Uh-oh," he muttered, "looks like your plugs are fouled up. I'll sure have to do this job on the double. Once the tide turns, we'll be in real trouble. Believe me, I don't want to face the current down by Lookout Point without your help, Skeeter, old boy."

Taking advantage of the lull at the peak of the tide, Bob worked frantically. He quickly removed the plugs and cleaned them.

"That's better, Skeeter, my friend," he whispered. "Now I'll get the plugs back in again, and we'll be ready to start."

Bob quickly inserted one plug into place. But just at the moment he reached for the other plug, the drifting boat swung broadside into a wave. Bob staggered for a moment. Then his foot caught under the fishing pole that he always carried in his boat. He sprawled across the bottom of the boat, his head and arms hanging over the side. With a look of disbelief he watched the bubbles rise to the surface as the spark plug zigzagged farther and farther down into the murky water.

"That did it," he moaned. "That fixed everything just great."

The breeze that had been blowing softly through Bob's hair seemed to quicken a little.

"It's good that the tide is beginning to go out now, Skeet," Bob murmured. "And if that wind keeps up, maybe I can steer the boat over near enough to Lookout Point to get some help from Jay and Sally. The way I see it, my biggest problem is to signal them soon enough so that they can be prepared."

Bob raised his hand to his mouth, put his first two fingers between his teeth, and blasted a shrill whistle that they had always used to signal one another. Quickly, he removed his shirt. Cutting two lengths of cord from his fishing line, he tied the shirt-sleeves to the pole at half-mast as a signal of distress.

"Now then, this should help," Bob muttered as he wedged the pole into the space between the backboard and the motor and tied it securely.

Bob guided the boat by shifting the motor's rudder at the stern. Taking advantage of the wind and tide, he was able to keep the boat from drifting too fast toward the Point.

Every few minutes Bob's whistle cut the air. Each one sounded more urgent than the last.

The speed of the boat quickened as it reached the beginning of the channel. Then Jay and Sally appeared on the Point, waving frantically to let him know they understood.

Time was short. Bob's boat was nearing the Point. He could feel the strong pull of the current.

"Keep your fingers crossed, Skeeter," he pleaded. "This is it."

Jay and Sally used their weight to bend down a long, thin branch of a tree by the water's edge. But as Bob reached high in the air and grasped the tip of the branch, there was a cracking sound .

"Look out!" Sally shouted. "The branch is breaking off from the tree."

Sally and Jay watched helplessly as the wind and current sent Bob and his boat out into the open sea.

"Bob, Bob!" Sally yelled "What can we do to help you? What should we do?"

"Call the harbor patrol!" he shouted. "I'll try for the red buoy."

The wind was brutal now, tearing at Bob's shirt hanging from the pole and sending a drenching spray of salt water into the boat.

Bob managed to guide the boat in the general direction of the red buoy. But as he drew near, he realized he was going to miss it by about four or five feet. Quickly, Bob made a frantic effort to catch onto the buoy.

"I've almost got it, Skeeter," he whispered.

Suddenly, a sharp gust of wind spun the boat from under Bob's feet. He lost his balance and fell into the water near the buoy. "Good-bye, Skeeter, old buddy," he murmured. "I hope the Coast Guard gets here in time to help us."

Bob struggled to reach the buoy, fighting the angry waters. He was able to remove his shoes and could swim better.

Slowly, inch by inch, he neared the buoy, which was bobbing up and down like an apple in a dunking tub. He gave one last lunge forward, and his arms grasped the buoy. Wearily, he rested his cheek against the cold metal. The water pulled at him, and for a moment he felt tears coming to his eyes.

Then he heard the reassuring siren of the harbor patrol and saw the boat coming toward him. Soon Bob was in the boat, shivering but grateful.

But what had happened to Skeeter? Bob wondered. About that time, he heard another siren. He looked back. A short distance away another boat had his skiff in tow. Bob sighed happily and murmured, "Well done, Skeeter. We're both all right now."

THE
SHORTCUT

By Margaret Springer

"Your attention, please, for the following announcement."

Dan and the other sixth-graders listened.

"A snow emergency has been declared. There's a bad storm on the way, and we want everyone home before it hits."

Dan looked at the gray sky outside. It didn't look much like a storm. It was hardly snowing.

"The buses are outside. If you live in town, senior students will escort the younger ones, as usual. Meet your snow buddies in their homerooms."

Dan sighed. His snow buddy was Mikey—the biggest chatterbox in kindergarten.

"This is fun, isn't it, Dan?"

Mikey wobbled as he aimed his feet into his boots. Dan helped him zip up his snowsuit, find his hat, pull his hood up over it, and tie the strings.

"Where's your scarf and mittens?"

Mikey shrugged. "Somewhere." They looked everywhere.

"Borrow from the lost-and-found box for now," Mikey's teacher said.

They were the last ones outside. The buses had left. Teachers hurried to their cars. The custodian locked up behind them. "Go straight home now," he said. "That storm's moving in fast."

Wind slapped at the flag on the flagpole. Thin sheets of snow blew sideways, blurring the sidewalk.

The long way home was left down Maple Street, then left along Wellington, and left again up Cedar Crescent. But Dan always took the path across the school field. It wound down the hill and came out at Cedar, right near Mikey's house. Dan could see it and his own house farther along.

"Let's take the shortcut," Dan said, taking Mikey's hand. "That snow is getting heavier."

Mikey stopped often to chatter or to catch snowflakes on his tongue.

They were partway down the hill when a sudden roaring wind hit. It sounded like huge trucks passing by. Everything was white.

"Wow! That's a big wind!" Mikey shouted.

"It's just snow blowing off the hill," said Dan, trying to sound sure.

They pushed ahead. Snow stung their faces. Dan squinted into the blurry whiteness. Whiteouts usually cleared after a while, but this one seemed permanent.

"I'm glad I'm with you," Mikey said. "You know the way."

But Dan wasn't sure they were still on the path. He couldn't see the houses. He hesitated and turned. Now he couldn't see the school, either. He couldn't see anything.

"Are we lost?" Mikey's voice was high.

"Of course not."

Dan tried not to think of blizzard stories he'd heard. People wandering in circles, lost. Or that farmer last winter, who died between his house and his barn. How could weather change so quickly?

The wind was in one direction now, howling fierce and strong. Mikey was having trouble staying on his feet.

"It's not very far," Dan said. *Don't panic,* he told himself. *Think.*

He tried to visualize the school grounds on a sunny day—the playground behind the school, then the long slope down toward the fence.

Yes! The fence! It went all around the school property, with a gate at Cedar. If they walked in a straight line in any direction they'd have to reach the fence.

"Come on." Dan held firmly to Mikey's mittened hand and turned slightly to let the wind blow them in a straight line. Sure enough, they reached the fence and were soon groping their way along it.

"We'll find the gate, and then we're home," Dan said happily.

But they didn't come to a gate. Maybe they were going in the other direction.

Mikey started to cry. "I'm cold." His scarf drooped below his chin.

"There's someone!" A blurry shape loomed in front of them. "Hey!" Dan called. Then he realized what it was. Playground equipment. A red slide. A yellow climber.

That meant they had gone the wrong way along the fence. They were almost back to school again, and the school would be locked and empty.

Worse, on this midwinter afternoon the light was beginning to fade.

"I'm cold," Mikey whimpered.

We could go back along the fence to the gate,
Dan thought. *But that's directly into the wind.*

Their scarves and mittens were soaked from the
wet snow. Dan's face felt numb. He knew they
risked frostbite if they stayed outside much
longer. The blizzard howled around them.

"Mikey," he said desperately. "We need shelter,
but I don't know what to do."

"We could go into the playhouse," Mikey said.

"The playhouse! I'd forgotten about that!"

They stumbled over to the playhouse, next to
the slide, and huddled inside.

Out of the wind, it felt almost warm. Mikey was
shaking with cold. Dan put his arms around him.
"Let's pretend we're polar bears," Dan said.

"Our mommies will be worried," Mikey whined.

"Don't worry. They'll come looking for us,"
Dan said. "I'll teach you some polar bear songs.
'Wiggle, wiggle, wiggle your hands hands hands.
Wiggle, wiggle, wiggle your feet feet feet. Wiggle,
wiggle, wiggle your legs legs legs.'"

"'Wiggle, wiggle, wiggle my nose nose nose!'"
shouted Mikey.

They sang songs. They kept moving. Dan knew
they mustn't fall asleep. He made sure they had
air as the snow drifted around the playhouse.

"Sing another polar bear song," Mikey said.

It was pitch dark when they heard the sound of snowmobiles and saw lights through the snow.

They leaped out of the playhouse. "Over here!" Dan shouted.

"Thank goodness! They're safe!"

Strong arms wrapped them in blankets and scooped them on board. The snowmobile bumped and loudly roared through the snow toward home.

"We played polar bears," Mikey said. "Dan is smart. He found the fence."

"Mikey is smart, too," said Dan, smiling. "He found the playhouse."

"We're good snow buddies," said Mikey.

"Yes," said Dan. "But that was definitely *not* a good shortcut!"

Night
of the
Big Wind

By Judy Cox

Marilee waved to Mrs. Smith as the car pulled out of the driveway. "Good-bye!" she called. "Don't worry about a thing!" The wind sent a garbage can lid clattering down the street. Marilee turned to Aimee and Andee, the four-year-old twins she was baby-sitting. A heavy weight seemed to settle on her shoulders.

For weeks she had begged to baby-sit. "I'm old enough," she told her mom. "And I've had the Red Cross baby-sitting class." Finally Mom agreed.

And now—her first job. She'd wanted it for so long. She wasn't about to admit she was nervous.

"What shall we do now, girls?" she asked brightly. Aimee's lower lip quivered, and her eyes filled with tears.

"I want my mommy," she whimpered. Andee looked on with disdain.

"She's a crybaby," she said coolly. "I want to watch T.V. Our other baby-sitter let us watch anything we want." Marilee knew this was true. The other baby sitter got fired—that's why Marilee had the job. She wasn't going to make the same mistake. Marilee picked up Aimee and carried her inside. Andee trailed along behind.

"Your mom will be home soon," said Marilee. "She just had to run some errands." Outside, the wind picked up. Suddenly there was a loud *CRASH!*

"What was that!" cried Aimee.

Marilee ran to the window to look. "Just a branch falling down," she giggled. "Nothing to worry about. I know what! I'll read a story." Aimee stopped crying. Andee smiled. Marilee settled the twins next to her on the couch and began to read. "Once upon a time there were four little rabbits," she began.

"Flopsy, Mopsy, and Cotton-tail!" yelled the twins in unison, bouncing up and down.

"And Peter," reminded Marilee. The wind moaned around the house like a restless ghost. Pinecones thudded against the window. Marilee pulled the twins closer and read louder. Aimee put her thumb in her mouth.

All afternoon the wind howled. Mrs. Smith didn't come home. Marilee read until she was hoarse. They played eight games of Candyland, and still Mrs. Smith didn't come. The sky grew dark. She turned on the lights. The hour hand of the clock crept around to seven o'clock. Mrs. Smith had been gone since three. Four hours!

"I'm hungry," whined Aimee. "I want my mommy now!"

"Me, too." Andee glared at Marilee as if it were her fault.

Marilee thought quickly. "Let's play Peter Rabbit!" she said. "I'll be Flopsy. Aimee, who will you be?"

"I'll be Mopsy!" yelled Andee, jumping up and down excitedly.

Aimee took her thumb out of her mouth and considered. Finally, she answered, "Cotton-tail."

"But who will be Peter?" demanded Andee. "I don't want to play a stupid old game! I'm hungry!"

The phone rang. It was Marilee's mother. "She's not home yet, Mom, and the twins are hungry." Marilee was hungry, too, and tired. She followed her mother's advice and made them all peanut butter sandwiches.

They finished the last bite when Marilee heard a weird noise. She opened the curtains and peered into the darkness. A fir tree in the back-yard whipped back and forth in the wind, hitting the high-tension power lines behind the house. Everytime the tree hit, two lines snapped together with a loud buzz, like the drone of an angry bee. A shower of orange sparks shot into the sky.

"What's happening?" asked Andee. The twins pressed close to each other, staring into the stormy night. Marilee looked down at their white faces and back at the tree. Sparks flew over the roof. What should she do? If only Mrs. Smith would come home!

"I'm scared!" Aimee began to sob. She wrapped her arms around Marilee's legs. The fir tree hit the lines again and more sparks erupted into the sky.

"Fire!" shrieked Andee. Marilee raced for the phone. Should she call her mother? Should she call the fire department?

"Will our house burn down?" Aimee cried.

With trembling fingers Marilee pushed 911. She swallowed hard when the operator answered and quickly told him the address. As soon as Marilee finished, there was a tremendous

BOOM! and the lights went out. The phone in her hand went dead.

The house was black. The twins clung to Marilee, whimpering. The wind roared in the trees and slammed against the house like a freight train. Marilee ran to the window, followed by the sobbing girls. Sparks sprayed into the sky and rained into the bushes by the street. Would the fire department come? And where, oh where, was Mrs. Smith?

She knelt to hold the twins in her arms. "Don't worry, girls. I'm here. I'll take care of you." She wished her own mother were here. Mom always knew what to do. "Let's be Flopsy, Mopsy, and Cotton-tail again!"

"And Peter," added Andee with a sniff. "You forgot Peter." There was an acrid smell of smoke in the air. What if an electric line fell down? Would the house catch fire? Marilee knew that she had to get the children to safety.

"We'll all be Peter," she said, "sneaking away from Mr. McGregor." She helped the twins feel their way through the dark house to the closet and pull on their coats. Outside, the wind pressed against her like a fist. She clutched the twins' hands in hers.

"Come along, bunnies!" she called gaily.

They stepped off the porch and onto the side-walk. Just at that moment a car turned into the driveway. Mrs. Smith was home.

"The roads were closed! I couldn't get through!" Mrs. Smith hugged the twins. A siren wailed in the distance. The fire engine was on its way. Mrs. Smith smiled at Marilee. "I knew I could count on you," she said.

Marilee's heart slowly stopped pounding. Her first baby-sitting job! If she could handle this, she could handle anything.

Danger
on the
Trail

By Marjorie Jorgensen

"Coming with me today, son?"

Brad Nelson shook his head without answering. He wanted to go—desperately—to be brave, and to be close to Lars Johnson, his new stepfather. But he couldn't.

Brad had never told anyone of his agonizing fear of heights. He saw the pained twist of his stepfather's lips. Then Lars mounted his horse, Diamond, and slowly rode off into the wet and windy morning.

Brad went indoors. His mother, writing entries in a ledger, smiled at him. In this year of 1897 their kitchen housed a branch Post Office. She was the post mistress. Lars carried the mail on horseback to the settlement just beyond the Cape. Brad had never gone with him.

A dangerous half-mile of the trail rounded the high rocky headland of Windy Cape. Lars said Diamond had left patches of hair on the cliff as she pressed close to it in fear of falling into the ocean below. One year a horse and its rider had been swept off the ledge in a storm.

Brad and his mother were eating their noon meal when Dr. Tucker hammered on the door and stepped into the kitchen.

"Mrs. Johnson, these powders need to be delivered to the doctor at the settlement today! Possibility of typhoid there."

Brad's mother looked shocked. "But Lars left a long time ago, Doctor."

"The boy will have to catch up to him then. I'd go, but Carrie's baby is overdue, and I don't dare leave her."

"No!" Brad said as his heart leaped in protest, and he swallowed a familiar sick feeling.

Dr. Tucker paid no attention. He laid the packet of powders and the postage on the counter and then hurried out, flinging a quick thank-you over his shoulder.

"Brad, saddle Lady." His mother was hauling out his sou'wester hat and Mackinaw jacket. "I'm putting the medicine in your pocket."

When she spoke with that firmness, Brad knew there was no arguing. On the road he put Lady to a gallop. Maybe he could catch Lars before he reached the Cape.

Where the wagon road curved inland, the trail to the settlement angled up through salal and huckleberry brush. Lady lunged and snorted as she leaned into the slope, scrambling on pebbles that rolled under her feet. The bushes whipped against Brad's legs in the stiff breeze.

They came out of the brush suddenly. A gust of wind hit with fury, tearing at Brad's hat and jacket. He hauled back on Lady's reins, his heart beating a tattoo in his throat. In front of him lay a narrow rock ledge barely three feet wide. Gouged out of a towering cliff, the top of the ledge was lost in misty fog and seemed to disappear as it rounded the Cape.

Brad looked down. Far below, the heaving gray swells of the Pacific seemed to pull him toward them. He dismounted in haste, his head whirling, and dropped flat on the ground.

Lady was nuzzling his hat. He didn't want to open his eyes, but he must. Something was not right. He raised his head, forcing himself to look.

Lars was sitting, unmoving, out there on the trail, at the point where it curved into nowhere!

"Father!" Brad yelled. "Here's another delivery Can you come and get it?" The wind ripped his cry into useless shreds. "Father, I can't come out to you!" Brad cried.

But he had to. Something told him that if he didn't go to him, Lars would fall off the Windy Cape Trail. *He must have the typhoid, too,* Brad thought. He forced himself to stand. Grasping Lady's reins, he tethered the horse to a sturdy vine on the side of the cliff. Then, dropping to his knees, he crawled onto Windy Cape Trail.

He focused his gaze close in front of him, willing himself not to look out or down. Foot by foot, Brad inched forward.

At long last, woolen pants and a pair of boots came into the edge of his vision. Brad raised his eyes. Lars's face was red, his gaze fogged and uncertain. Beyond him, Diamond stood patiently.

"I'm sick," Lars whispered. "Stay back."

Brad hesitated, then said, "Father, you need help. I have to come near you to get Diamond and send her on to the settlement for help, OK?"

Lars nodded faintly. Brad gripped his stepfather's shoulder and cautiously stood up.

"Whoa, Diamond," he said softly. He stepped across Lars's stretched-out legs and took hold of the horse's tail, then grabbed the back of her saddle. He wrote a note on the packet of powders and slipped it into the mail pouch. Reaching forward, he secured Diamond's dragging reins.

"It's up to you, girl," Brad said, giving Diamond a soft pat. With a sigh she moved forward along the edge of the trail. The settlement was barely visible at the far end.

There was nothing to do but wait for Diamond and help to return. Brad sat down beside his stepfather and slipped a hand comfortingly into his. Out over the ocean, the feeble sun laid a patch of light on the water.

A Little
Know-How

By Elizabeth Weiss Vollstadt

"Sorry, J.J.," said her dad as he put his fishing gear in the little boat, "but I want some peace and quiet. I do not want to untangle your lines all day. Nor do I want bait all over the bottom of the boat because you can't sit still."

"But Dad, I didn't mean to knock over the bucket. It's just that I figured out a great dance step to this tune and had to try it." With that, J.J. whipped a harmonica out of the back pocket of her bright pink shorts and started to play a bouncy melody.

The red flowers on her big straw hat bobbed up and down to the tune.

"And as for that harmonica . . ." J.J.'s dad shook his head as he untied the lines. "All that noise probably scared the fish. No, I'm going alone." He started the engine and glided away from the dock.

J.J. stopped playing and watched the boat cut through the clear, blue water. What a perfectly awful vacation this was turning out to be! What was the fun of being on an island in Maine if you were stuck on shore? She made an about-face and bumped into Sammie Lou, owner of the Blue Shutters Motel, where J.J. and her parents were staying.

"Whoa," said Sammie Lou. "You don't want to fall on those stones." She nodded her gray head at the empty boat slip. "No fishin' today?"

"Dad won't take me," said J.J. She blurted out the story of yesterday's disaster. "I can't do anything right!"

"Nonsense," said Sammie Lou. "All you need is some slowin' down—and a little know-how. How about fishin' with me today? Come on. Let's go ask your mom."

Fifteen minutes later they were at Sammie Lou's favorite fishing spot. "Watch what I do," she said. She picked up a fishing rod. Her line flew as gracefully as the gulls that soared overhead.

"Now you try," she said.

J.J. swung her rod. The hook stuck in the cushion behind her. She tried again. This time it plopped into the water, right next to the boat. And again. The line tangled in the canvas top that shaded them from the sun.

J.J. figured she had tried at least a hundred times. Then, on one hundred and one, she had it right. "Good job!" said Sammie Lou as she reached into the bait bucket.

The two friends fished quietly from the stern of the boat. Soon J.J. felt a bite, and with Sammie Lou's help, she reeled in her first sea bass.

They fished for another hour before Sammie Lou pointed to a dark cloud over the ocean. "That sure doesn't look friendly," she said. "We'd better head home."

She stood up and started toward the bow of the boat to pull up the anchor. Just then, a large motor boat roared past, making sudden waves in the glassy water. Their boat began to bob crazily.

Sammie Lou reached out to grab the canvas top but was too late. She lost her balance and fell. Seconds later she was lying on the deck, holding her right arm. Her face was white with pain.

"I've hurt my shoulder," she gasped. She pulled herself onto the seat and sat very still.

J.J. looked around frantically for help, but no boats were nearby.

"You . . . have . . . to . . . get . . . us . . . back," Sammie Lou said slowly, as if each word were an effort.

"But I can't . . . ," J.J. started to say, then stopped. They couldn't just sit here. Sammie Lou looked awful. And that dark cloud seemed closer.

"OK," she said in a shaky voice. "What do I do first?"

"Pull up the anchor. The line is in the bow."

J.J. started pulling, but the anchor didn't budge. She looked at Sammie Lou and at the approaching storm. "It's no use," she wailed, ready to drop the line and give up.

Then, taking a deep breath, she tugged one last time. The anchor came free with a jerk. J.J. fell onto the seat. "I did it!" she yelled.

The breeze felt colder now. J.J.'s hands shook when she turned the key to start the engine. Her heart beat faster when the engine roared.

"Good," said Sammie Lou. "Now move the handle forward just a little until the boat starts movin'. Then you can add speed."

J.J. moved the lever. Nothing happened. She pushed harder. The boat leaped forward. Panicked, J.J. pushed the handle back, stalling the engine. Tears came to her eyes as the thunder rumbled closer.

J.J. swallowed hard and tried again. Slowly, the boat started to move. Lightning lit up the dark sky. Thunder boomed like a mighty cannon. J.J. slowly pushed the lever forward and held the wheel tightly as the boat raced through the swelling waves.

Large, heavy raindrops were falling as they approached the Blue Shutters Motel. J.J. could see her father on the dock. He ran to the boat just as J.J. turned off the engine and glided into the dock with a thump.

"Thank heavens you're safe!" he shouted. He jumped into the boat and took J.J. in his arms. Then he saw Sammie Lou. Her eyes were shut in pain. "What happened?"

"I fell," Sammie Lou said. "I'm sure glad J.J. was with me. I never would've made it back alone. That girl of yours is a real hero—she has some know-how!"

J.J. could see the surprise in her father's eyes turn to pride. "How about another chance at fishing with me?" he said to her with a grin. "Who knows—maybe I'll need some of that know-how."

J.J. whirled around with delight. Then the thunder clapped again. Startled, she slipped and fell on the wet deck. She looked at her father, but he was busy helping Sammie Lou to her feet.

The rain poured down in sheets as they slowly made their way to the motel office. But J.J. bounced along to a cheery melody only she could hear.

Deer Patrol

By Joe Ewing

Early on Saturday morning Trevor Collins walked into the ranger station of the United States Forest Service. "Wow! It's cold out there," he said as he stomped the snow from his boots. Suddenly, he stopped and stared. His father and Assistant Ranger Blake were sitting in their chairs, ears glued to the radio.

"Dad, what is it? What's wrong?" asked Trevor. His dad motioned for him to sit down and be quiet. Trevor slid into a chair and watched the worried looks on the faces of his father and Ranger Blake.

The ring of the telephone startled Trevor. His father, Ranger Collins, picked it up and listened carefully. "Oh, no! How much did you say?" he asked. After listening a moment longer, he slowly hung up the phone.

"Dad, will you please tell me what's going on?" asked Trevor.

His father turned toward him. "Do you remember that deer herd we were hunting for last week? The one we lost just after the first big snow of the season? Well, we've been unable to find it. We have all the rangers out now looking for it, so we can get some feed to the deer. They can't last very long without food. That phone call just told me that another fifteen inches of snow is due before nightfall. But worst of all, Dave Bennington hasn't been heard from in twelve hours. The last time he radioed, he told us he was in that canyon up near Ridge Road. We think his truck may have slid over the bank and down into the lake. I'm getting ready now to go up and see if I can find him."

"Dad," said Trevor, "I want to go along. I'm old enough now. Please, can I go."

"OK, Trevor, grab your snowshoes, and let's get to the truck."

Trevor ran to the garage, grabbed his snow-shoes, and raced back to the truck.

His dad was already in the driver's seat and had the motor running. He put the truck into four-wheel drive and slowly left the ranger station. They turned up the fire trail leading toward Ridge Road. They drove in silence, concentrating on keeping the truck moving on the trail. In many places the drifts were three feet high.

"Hang on, Trevor," his dad shouted over the roar of the motor. "This next drift's going to be a tough one." Swiftly shifting into low gear, Ranger Collins raced the engine and the truck broke through. "We won't make it through another one like that," he said. "But we'll go as far as we can and then leave the truck."

After another mile they pulled into a clearing. "We'll stop here," his dad said. "Let's get out the snowshoes."

Quickly, Trevor and his father strapped on the snowshoes and continued up the trail. They plodded along, keeping a sharp lookout for the missing truck.

Suddenly, Trevor stopped and pointed toward the lake. "Look, Dad, over there. I see the truck!"

His father ran to the bank where Trevor was standing. "You're right," he said. "Let's go!"

They hurried down the steep bank, slipping and sliding in the deep snow. When they reached the lake, Trevor exclaimed, "Boy! It's lucky that ice is thick. The truck would have sunk, otherwise. Come on, Dad, let's see if Dave is in the cab."

They ran over to the truck and opened the door. The driver was nowhere in sight.

"What could have happened to him?" Trevor asked. "Where could he be?"

"I don't know," his father responded. "But I'll bet if we follow these tracks across the lake, we'll find him."

Trevor and his father started in the direction that the tracks pointed.

"Dad," cried Trevor, "it looks as if he fell down."

Sure enough, the marks in the snow told the story. Ranger Bennington had fallen and stayed down for a few minutes before continuing across the lake.

"I can't figure it out," said Trevor. "He must have been dragging something."

"He was," answered his father. "And he was limping, too, as you can tell from the tracks. He must have hurt himself when the truck went over the bank."

The sky was getting darker. Trevor and his father hurried on as fast as the snowshoes would let them. They wanted to find Dave before the storm hit. Reaching the other side of the lake, they struggled up the steep bank and looked out on a little clearing at the edge of the woods.

"There he is!" shouted Trevor.

"And there's the deer herd, too," answered his father. "He must have spotted the herd just before his truck went over the bank. He dragged one bale of hay clear across the lake so the deer could have some food. We'll help him with the rest of the hay now."

At that moment Dave looked up and waved. He got up and limped slowly across the field toward them.

"Trevor, go back to the truck and radio a message to headquarters," said Ranger Collins. "I'll find a sapling and cut a crutch, then help Dave across the lake. Hurry, now. The storm is almost here. And thanks, Trevor. You've been a big help today."

The Rescue
OF THE
Golden Mermaid

By Thelma Anderson

Sarah and Linda Martin stood by the house, watching the river a quarter of a mile away. Two weeks of rainy weather had made the South Dakota countryside wet and soggy.

"Wow!" Sarah said to her younger sister. "Look at that river!" The muddy water was lapping over the banks, sending long fingers of water all across the lowlands.

The telephone rang, and the girls ran into the house. Sarah hurried to answer it.

"We've had a cloudburst here," said Bill Johnson, their closest neighbor, who lived ten miles upriver. "Rained five inches in about an hour. Tell your dad if he has any livestock on the lowlands, he'd better move them to higher ground." The receiver clicked as he hung up.

"The river is going to flood, Linda," Sarah said, looking worried. "And Princess Whitefoot is in the river pasture!"

The girls ran outside and looked toward the pasture half a mile to the south. They could often see their palomino mare grazing on the flat in a bend of the river, but she was not in sight now. The little streams of water they had been watching had already turned into what looked like small lakes, with only a few islands of higher ground pointing up above the water.

"I wish Mom and Dad were home," Linda said.

"But they aren't," Sarah said. "And by the time they get back from town, it'll be too late. We'll have to get Princess Whitefoot out of the pasture."

The girls ran to the barn and got a bridle. Then they headed down the hill and across the soggy cornfield, their feet sinking deeply into the soft mud with each step.

"It's odd that we can't see her," Sarah said. "I wonder where she is?"

"Since the flat is covered with water, she may have gone under the trees on one of those high spots," Linda answered.

The girls reached the pasture gate, and Sarah threw it open. They walked to the water's edge and scanned the vast sea of water.

"Hey, Princess Whitefoot, where are you?" Sarah called. "Here, Princess." She whistled, the shrill sound carrying across the water. An answering nicker came from a clump of trees on a small hill.

"Come here, Princess," Sarah urged. Again came the nicker but still no sight of the mare.

"Why doesn't she come?" Linda asked. "The water is getting deeper every minute. Look behind us. It's starting across the field now."

"Maybe she's afraid of the water, or maybe she's caught on something," Sarah said. "We'll have to go over and get her."

Quickly, the girls waded into the water. Soon it sloshed over their knees, then grew shallower as they reached the island.

"Well, look at that!" Linda exclaimed. "Aren't you cute!"

"So that's why you wouldn't come," Sarah said.

The mare nickered anxiously. Her great, gentle eyes held a worried expression as she touched her tiny new foal with her nose.

Sarah slipped the bridle over the mare's head. The little foal reached out its inquisitive nose to touch Linda's hand.

"Hey, that tickles," Linda laughed.

"We'd better get out of here," Sarah said.

She swung on Princess Whitefoot's back, then pulled Linda up behind her. Princess Whitefoot stepped into the water with the tiny foal pressed close to her side. The foal stopped knee-deep in water and nickered. Princess Whitefoot nickered in reply, urging her baby to follow. But the little foal, afraid of the water, refused to move.

The mare turned back and stood beside her foal. Coaxingly, she pushed the foal into the water with her head, then walked beside it. The foal pressed close to the mare's side as it walked into deeper water. The rapidly rising water was soon over the mare's knees and touching the little foal's belly.

"Look!" Linda exclaimed. "The field we just came across is covered with water."

The water rose higher until it was washing against the mare's sides, and the tiny foal had to swim. The force of the current started to carry it away.

"Whoa!" Sarah shouted, sliding into the water and grabbing the foal's neck. She braced herself against the force of the water as she stood waist-deep, holding the little horse.

"Reach down and unsnap a bridle rein, Linda, quick!" she said.

Linda unsnapped the rein and handed it to Sarah. Sarah looped the rein around the foal's body, over its withers, and behind its front legs.

"Guide her straight for the gate, Linda," she said as she wrapped the rein around one hand and grabbed the mare's tail with the other. "I'll hang on."

They moved ahead. The rapidly rising water soon forced the mare to swim, pulling Sarah and the colt behind her. She swam steadily until suddenly her feet hit solid ground. They splashed across the field in water knee-deep, then climbed the hill to the house.

"Good girl, Princess," Sarah said. "I'm sure glad that's over, and I'll bet you are, too." The mare nudged her foal with her nose.

The little foal pressed close to its mother as they went to the barn, where the girls rubbed the wet foal with dry rags.

"Isn't she a little beauty?" Linda said. "She's going to be a golden palomino, just like her mother. What should we name her?"

"I know a good name," Sarah laughed. "Let's call her the Golden Mermaid."

"Yes, let's," Linda said. "That's a good name for a water baby."

Nothing to Write About

By Myra Sanderman

"Bobby went three for three!" Stoney said to his mom, running into the kitchen to show her the postcard.

"Is that good?" she asked.

"It's great. Three hits in three at-bats." He groaned. "But I have nothing to write him about."

"You love watching Chris feed the pelicans," she said. Chris was a fisherman who lived nearby.

"I wrote that already."

"How about the things Chris taught you?"

Stoney rolled his eyes. "That's just some old signaling stuff from when he was in the navy."

Stoney hadn't been happy since his dad had taken over managing the Marlin Lodge fishing resort in the Florida Keys. It was only for the summer. But this summer he was supposed to go to sports camp back in Chicago with his friends from fifth grade.

Stoney walked out to the dock. "If your face gets any longer, you're going to trip over it," Chris called.

Stoney kicked at a pebble.

Chris eased into his small boat. "Give me a hand with the painter, will you?"

Stoney knew that Chris meant the rope hitching the dinghy to the pier. Chris was always telling him things and then testing Stoney to see if he remembered.

"Come on out with me," Chris said. "I've got crackers so you can feed the parrot fish."

"Nothing else to do," Stoney said. He checked with his mom, then ran back to the boat.

Chris hunched over the outboard, pulling the starter cord until the motor finally caught. He eased the boat out of the harbor.

The resort was on the Gulf of Mexico. Stoney liked the way the water turned from light green to a dark, blue-jeans kind of blue as it got deeper.

Suddenly the motor sputtered, then stopped.

"What's up?" Stoney asked.

"Beats me," Chris said. "Throw out that anchor so we can hold our position."

Chris pulled the motor's cord again and again, sweat beading on his forehead like little marbles. "Got to rest," he said.

"I'll try," said Stoney. "Hey, Chris, you don't look so good."

The old man's eyes were closed. His skin was drawn and chalky.

"You OK?" Stoney asked.

Chris opened his eyes. "Hurts," he said, pointing to his chest.

"Your heart?"

Chris closed his eyes again. "Rest . . . ," he managed to say.

Stoney helped Chris lean back against the extra life jackets. Then he tried to start the engine. Chris had taught him how.

Ten, twelve hard pulls. Nothing.

They were pretty far out. Could he row back?

Chris moaned. An icy feeling snaked up Stoney's back, and he shivered despite the blazing sun.

Stoney sat down to think. His watch said noon. His dad would come looking for them if they hadn't come in by supper. But could Chris wait?

Before Stoney could ask, he heard a muffled sound of a motor. Maybe it was a Coast Guard boat! Chris had told him they sometimes patrolled these waters.

"Help! Over here!" Stoney shouted, waving his arms. But the other boat sped by, too far away for its wake to even rock Chris's boat.

Stoney stared down and wiped his hands on his shorts. They had been bright red and yellow when he put them on this morning. Now they were streaked with grease and sticking to him like a wet washcloth.

Red and yellow. What had Chris told him about those colors?

The red and yellow flags Chris used in the navy to send messages! Stoney clapped his hands. Now if he could only remember the signals for help.

Stoney pulled off his shorts, life jacket, and T-shirt. Standing carefully, he took the shorts in one hand and the shirt in the other. He took a deep breath and began to signal.

"*S*, right hand straight out from your side. Left hand down, angled out from your side," he said aloud. Was that it?

"*O*, right hand angled up from your shoulder. Left hand straight across your chest."

"*S*." Would anybody see?

Stoney brought his arms down in front of him. He was sure that meant a space between messages.

S . . . O . . . S, Stoney signaled. Again. *S . . . O . . . S.*

"Chris, am I doing it right?" Stoney heard only the sound of the waves lapping against the boat. Chris was barely breathing. Would he make it?

A hum caught Stoney's attention, and he searched in the direction of the noise. A boat was coming toward them! Stoney waved his shorts and shirt wildly as the Coast Guard cutter approached.

"Are you all right?" one of the crew called.

"It's him," said Stoney. "I think . . . his heart . . . " Stoney was suddenly very tired. He could barely answer the crew's questions as they helped him onto their boat.

"He's still alive," said one of the men helping to lift Chris, "but we'd better radio to have an ambulance meet us."

"Will he be OK?" Stoney asked.

"I think he will be," said the crewman. He covered Stoney with a light blanket. "We saw your signal. How did you know to do that?"

"Chris taught me . . . ," Stoney said, yawning, " . . . lots of neat things."

Stoney wrote Bobby a postcard about signaling for help, another one about visiting Chris in the hospital, and another about the big party they hoped to give Chris before the summer ended. Bobby wrote back.

"Bobby got his lifesaving certificate!" Stoney said, running into the kitchen where his mom was working. He waved the postcard under her nose. "Now what am I going to write about?"

His mother looked horrified.

"Just kidding," he said with a grin and ran out into the sun.

Under Pressure

By Bernadine Beatie

"This will be a curve," Phil said. He grinned down at four-year-old Judy Martin, rolled a baseball around in his hand, and sighted toward an old tire hanging from a tree limb.

Judy danced up and down with excitement. Of all the boys at her father's summer camp in the Rocky Mountains, Judy liked Phil best. She loved secrets, and only she knew that Phil came here alone each day to practice. She had promised to tell no one, not even her parents.

Phil threw, then smiled as the ball curved out, then sailed straight through the hole in the tire.

"Hey, that was some curve!" Dan Larson called out from behind Phil and Judy.

Phil turned, his face a blend of surprise and dismay. "It was an accident," he said. "I can't pitch!"

"You can too! You throw through the hole every time!" Judy piped up. Then she covered her mouth with her hand and looked guiltily at Phil.

Dan laughed. "I'll get my catcher's mitt, and we'll see. We sure need a pitcher if we're going to beat the team from Camp Clayton."

"No!" Phil said sharply. "I'm not going to play."

"Why not?" Dan asked, looking puzzled.

"I just can't!" Phil said and turned abruptly away. There was a dull, empty feeling in his stomach. If he explained, Dan wouldn't understand. Nobody did, not even Mr. Martin. Phil knew he was a good pitcher—good until the going got rough. Just let the bases get loaded, and something happened to him. He'd tense up every time, miss the plate a mile, or lob in soft, easy balls that anybody could hit. Phil frowned, remembering the two important games he had lost for his home team this spring.

At dinner that night, Nick Finley called out, "Hey, Phil, how about going out for the team?

Dan says you pitch a fast curve ball and that you have a strong arm."

"No!" said Phil. "I really don't, it was just luck the time he saw me."

"You could at least try," Dan said angrily.

Every boy at the table spoke up loudly, siding with Dan.

Mr. Martin tried to help Phil by changing the subject. "By the way, guys," he called out, "a couple of boys over at Camp Clayton saw some cougar tracks—big ones from what they said."

"They're always seeing something. Last year it was bear tracks," Dan said, shrugging. "That's not as important right now as finding a pitcher."

"That's right," a dozen voices called out.

Phil sat red-faced and miserable, shaking his head as the boys continued to plead and argue with him.

"That's enough, guys," Mr. Martin said finally. "Phil has the right to make up his own mind."

Phil pushed back from the table, excused himself, and left the room.

Even though he knew he would never pitch another game, Phil still practiced when he was alone. That was often now. For as the day of the game with Camp Clayton neared, the boys pointedly avoided Phil.

Two days before the game, Mr. Martin rapped on the table at breakfast. "We're going to ride up to Red Rock for a cookout. Mrs. Martin and Judy will take the food in the pickup and meet us there."

Phil's heart rose as cheers greeted Mr. Martin's announcement. A day away from camp might make the boys forget the baseball game. It seemed to, for when they saddled their horses and rode out, Dan called to Phil to ride beside him.

"Sure!" Phil agreed and grinned happily while Dan chattered as if they were still good friends.

The trail was rocky and steep. After a time they reached a scattering of pine trees, then topped a rise and sighted the pickup. It was parked beneath a rocky bluff on a narrow stretch of level ground. Dan pulled his pony to a stop.

"Phil," he said, "the guys want me to ask you one last time. Will you pitch for us?"

Phil's heart sank. "I can't, Dan," he said miserably, "I just can't."

"*Won't,* you mean." Dan whirled his horse and rode back to the others.

Later, when the boys decided to climb the bluff, Phil remained behind.

"Don't you want to go?" Mr. Martin asked.

Phil shrugged. "I'm going to take a walk. I'll be back soon."

"Suit yourself." Mr. Martin yawned. "I'm going to take a nap."

Judy darted toward Phil. "Take me!" she cried.

"No, Judy," Mrs. Martin said firmly. "It's nap time for you, too."

Phil walked slowly. Soon he found himself on an outcropping of rock overlooking the trail. He sat, telling himself he didn't care what Dan and the others thought. In a few weeks he would be home. But there was a dry, sick taste in his mouth. He did care; he cared a lot! Phil closed his eyes and leaned back. The sun was warm and after some time he fell asleep.

He was awakened by the sound of Mr. Martin's alarmed voice calling, "Judy! Judy!" Phil opened sleepy eyes and glanced at the trail below. He gasped in disbelief. He must be dreaming. Only in a dream would a small girl walk along a mountain trail, cuddling a cougar cub in her arms, while the mother cougar crept like an evil shadow behind her. But it wasn't a dream—it was real! Phil's body went weak with fright. What could he do? There was no time to get help. He had nothing to defend Judy with, nothing but a baseball.

Phil was pulling the baseball from his pocket as he rose. "Judy," he called out, "put down the kitty."

"No," Judy said. "It's my kitty. I found it."

When Judy stopped, the cougar stopped, too. Her tail twitched, then she crouched, body tensed to spring.

Phil didn't wait. He fixed his eyes on the cougar's shoulder, drew back his arm, and threw, just as Mr. Martin pounded up beside him. The ball sailed straight and true. It hit the exact center of the big cat's shoulder, making a dull thud.

The cougar snarled and whirled toward the new enemy as Judy looked over her shoulder. She gave a cry of fear and dropped the cub.

"Move away, Judy, slowly—slowly," her father ordered. But even as Mr. Martin spoke, the cougar snatched up her cub and, carrying it firmly between her teeth, bounded down the trail.

Mr. Martin and Phil skidded and slipped down the outcropping of rock. Mr. Martin gathered Judy into his arms.

"Don't ever tell me," Mr. Martin said shakily, looking up at Phil, "that you're no good under pressure!"

Suddenly, Phil was grinning, even though he felt a little shaky himself. "Mr. Martin," he said, "you're right. I know that now. A person doesn't ever really lose unless he quits trying."

"Then we'd better get going," said Mr. Martin. "You're pretty good, but a little practice before the game with Clayton won't hurt."